DEAD GIRLS DON'T CRY

J.M. GOODRICH

Dead Girls Don't Cry

Also By J.M. Goodrich

Deadly Celebrations

Emily's Wish

Snowflakes & Heartaches

Undying Love

Coming Home

Love Me Right

Summer Nights

Spirit And Soul

Bruised Heart

Just One Night

After All This Time

To Be Loved

Last Resort

Unexpected

A Promise Of Love

Dead Girls Don't Cry

Lana, Jade, and Rose are the best of friends, having bonded over their shared torment of being bullied and their secret fascination with witchcraft.
Desperate to reclaim their power, they gather in their secret hideout and attempt their very first spell - one against their bully.
However, instead of targeting their enemy, the spell leads to tragic consequences, claiming lives all around them.
As panic sets in, they discover a hidden warning within the spell's text. In their moment of fear, they discover that they may be the next target of their own magic.

ONE

"Hey Rose, do you still have that perfume I like? The one I borrowed the last time I was over?" Lana asked her friend.

She could hear objects being moved around through the speaker phone. They always spoke to each other on the phone every morning while getting ready for school. "I think so, let me check. The one in the blue bottle, right? Shaped sort of like a teardrop?"

"That's the one. If you find it, can I borrow it again, pretty please?"

She heard more rustling. "Found it!" Rose yelled triumphantly after a few minutes. "I'll bring it with me. You really should buy your own though."

Lana laughed. "Thanks, girl. I totally owe you one." She turned to Jade, who was sitting on her bed examining her nails. "You're right, I really should buy my own stuff. I'm always borrowing things from you guys," she shrugged. She hung up the phone and tossed it in her purse.

Jade looked up at her friend. "You know we don't mind," she smiled. "What's ours is yours. And I don't know about you," she said as she focused her attention back on her nails, "but I just don't feel like going to school today. We should totally ditch." She said, tucking her feet underneath her.

Jade never liked school. Who did though, honestly? It was pretty much a daily thing for her to suggest skipping school for the day. None of us ever went for it though.

"You know I would love to, but my parents would totally kill me," Lana answered, brushing out her long hair. She would never admit it, but Lana was a little terrified of breaking the rules. Especially ones set by her parents. She secretly wanted nothing more than to please the two of them, and the thought of breaking the rules and making them angry made her feel sick.

"I'm just so sick of Queen Veronica and her posse," she said, her voice dripping with disgust. "You'd think they could let up on the teasing just once. Just one day I would like to be able to walk around school and not have to worry about vicious rumors being started, or garbage being dumped on my head in the cafeteria, or dead animals being shoved in my locker." She shuddered at that last thought. The girls never retaliated in hopes that the torture would eventually stop, but there was no stopping Veronica.

"I know what you mean," Lana sighed. "She's never been nice, but this year she kicked up the bitchiness a few notches."

Jade laughed.

"This is our senior year though," Lana continued. "Maybe she'll cool off soon. Or at least find someone else to pick on for a while." The other girls wished they could be as hopeful as their friend.

"Doubt it. You know her, she's not happy until everyone around her is miserable. It's been that way since I've known her."

Lana drove both of her friends to school, as she was the

only one of their group who owned a car. They sat at their usual bench outside as they awaited the first morning bell.

"Do you guys have your costumes yet?" Rose asked, bouncing excitedly in her seat.

Jade took off her sunglasses to address her friend. "Don't you think we're a little too old to be dressing up?"

"You're never too old for Halloween," she shot back, looking slightly offended.

Lana just laughed as she laid in the sun, enjoying the unseasonable warmth.

"You freaks are too old for everything," an annoyed voice spoke.

Veronica stood before them with a sneer on her face. "And it's not like the three of you need a costume anyway. You're scary and freaky looking enough as it is." Her followers laughed. They automatically laughed at everything she said though, whether it truly was funny or not. Her so-called friends followed her blindly, never having an original thought of their own. Seriously, there was probably only one single brain cell among them.

The three of them stood there silently. They had learned not to engage Veronica in any sort of conversation. It wasn't worth it, she would always win. Or at the very least, that's what they would let her think. She was rude, hurtful, cold-hearted and cruel. But most of all, she was extremely annoying. No one enjoyed talking to her.

Veronica tossed her hair over her shoulder. "What's wrong? Black cat got your tongue?" She laughed again. She then leaned down, getting right in Lana's face. "The three of you will never be anything other than the nasty, disgusting freaks that you are. No one will ever accept you. No one will ever love you. You will be alone. Forever." She stared Lana in the eye, waiting for her to speak, to respond. She wanted her to hurt, to lash out. She wanted to see the pain in Lana's eyes.

But Lana refused to entertain her, so she bit her tongue and kept it all in. She wouldn't give her what she wanted.

Finally, she stood up, angry and annoyed. "Whatever. I'm done with you. Freaks." She added as she walked away, closely followed by her little minions.

"God, I hate her so much," Jade fumed once she was out of earshot.

"So do I," Lana replied, just as angry as her friend. "She needs to be taught a lesson. This has gone on long enough." She turned to her friends, eyes shining with ideas. "What do you say we meet up at the old house this weekend and come up with something extra special for her?"

"I like that idea," Rose smiled, wondering what exactly her friend had in mind.

"Count me in," Jade added, throwing one more look in Veronica's direction. "It's about time someone took that bitch down."

The three of them nodded, ready to take their revenge. Veronica bullied the entire school, though she focused most of her energy on Jade, Lana, and Rose. No one knew why. No one did anything about it though, either.

No one stood up to her, not even any adult around.

They would have to take matters into their own hands.

Two

Saturday couldn't come fast enough. The girls had spent everyday after school researching spells, looking for the perfect one to take care of their little bully problem.

They went out to their favorite place to hang out: an old abandoned house in the middle of the woods. It was rundown and kind of smelly, but it suited their needs perfectly. No one ever bothered them there. No one else even knew of its existence.

It was so old that the forest had already begun to reclaim it, and from the outside it just looked like an enormous mass of trees and moss at first glance. The girls had stumbled upon it by accident one night while wandering around the woods after having a little too much to drink.

After a while of them visiting with no interruptions they decided to just claim it as their own. Out here there was no one to bully them, no one to tease them or call them freaks. They were free to just be themselves. Out here they were free to work on their witchcraft, which they were all secretly very passionate about.

They had all stumbled upon witchcraft early last summer, and were instantly drawn to its dark, seductive power. It's what drew them to each other, and the three of them have been inseparable ever since. Nothing, and no one could tear them apart.

Lana picked up the other two girls since she was the only one who had a car, and they headed out to their secret spot. You could practically feel their excitement in the air. They had been studying witchcraft extensively since last year, but have yet to actually cast or perform a single spell.

This would be their very first.

When they arrived Rose set out a fresh bowl of food and water by the front door for Spirit, the black cat that occasionally hung around the house.

"Why don't you just formally adopt the thing?" Jade asked her.

Rose let out a sigh. "You know I'd love to, but my dad is deathly allergic to cats."

"Or so he says," she rolled her eyes.

"No, really, he is," Rose replied with a sharp nod. "I've been trying for years to get him to let me have a pet."

"Well, that's too bad then," shrugged Jade, bending down to pet the purring cat. Just as the girls had claimed the house, so did Spirit. He still ran off into the woods every once in a while, exploring for up to a few days at a time. But he always came back. The girls made sure he always had food, water, and a comfy place to sleep.

"Yeah, but old Spirit here is good enough for me. I still get to take care of and love the little guy." Rose smiled and led the way into the house.

Lana located the Book of Shadows containing all their spells while Jade lit a few candles around the room. They had them stashed all over the house, both for use in spells and for light since there was no electricity running out here.

The Book of Shadows was something that Lana had found tucked away in her attic. She didn't know who it belonged to originally, just that it had been someone in her family. On the cover was her family crest and her last name. But that was it, no first name or mention of anyone else's name found anywhere in the book. But every page was filled with spells, incantations, spell ingredients, and everything else they could ever need to perform a spell. Every inch of the book was filled in with tiny, cramped handwriting, making a lot of it nearly impossible to decipher.

Lana had been sitting at home one day, bored, when she felt something calling to her from the attic. The call was so strong after a while that she simply couldn't ignore it any longer. So up to the attic she went, snooping around until at last she located the book. She swore it just about vibrated at her touch, which was how she knew it was something special. That this was what had been calling to her.

It cemented the feeling she had about her being meant to be a witch and to study witchcraft. She found comfort and meaning in the texts, even if she didn't know what they meant.

The three best friends practiced in secret and swore to never tell another living soul about their newfound passion. No one would understand.

And they were teased enough as it was.

Each girl had their own personal, yet similar experiences that led them to believing in witchcraft and that it was what they were meant to do.

That it was a part of them.

Rose had been upset one day after being turned down yet about getting a family pet. She was always so gentle and nurturing. She just wanted a little puppy or kitty of her very own to love, care for, and always be there for her. Rose hated being alone, and longed for a little furry companion.

One night at dinner she was still upset. She sat down at the table, refusing to speak to her parents. She was through arguing and didn't want to cry in front of them. So she opted for the silent treatment.

Her parents tried only once to engage her in conversation before shrugging their shoulders and then simply ignoring her. As her mother made last minute preparations and began bringing the food to the table, Rose's anger began to build. This wasn't just about a pet. Her parents never seemed to listen to her, dismissing her wants and desires as nothing. She often felt unseen as well as unheard by her own parents. She hated feeling this way and closed her eyes, trying to steady her emotions.

Instead, she took two deep breaths before her eyes flew back open at the sound of her mother screaming in pain. The pot of mashed potatoes had somehow exploded directly in her face as she carried it to the table. It wasn't on the heat on the stove or anything. Her mother dropped what remained of the pot as she was struck with scolding potatoes and sharp, metal shards from the pot.

Rose sat there stunned as her father jumped up in an instant to help her mother. She couldn't hear a word her father said, and her mother's screams seemed to fade away. She just felt guilt, shame. She just knew that somehow she had been the cause of this, of her mother's pain. And it terrified her.

Since that incident she has worked harder to control her emotions. Rose never had any fits of anger after that and as a result, no more incidents. She was terrified of hurting her parents, or worse . . . accidently killing them. She couldn't bear the thought. So while she was at home she worked hard to regulate her emotions.

After the potato incident, she realized there was some-thing different about herself. Wanting answers, she began to research on her own what it could possibly be. Through this she discovered the world of magic and witchcraft.

Jade was out getting her hair done when her discovery took place. She arrived early to her appointment and after checking in, sat in the waiting room with a magazine. She could hear laughter coming from the two girls sitting across from her. She tried her best to ignore it, but they just kept getting louder and louder, as if trying to get her attention. When Jade finally looked up from the article she was reading the two girls stopped staring at her, falling off their chairs as they laughed even harder.

Jade rolled her eyes at their childish behavior. She felt second hand embarrassment just looking at the two of them sprawled out on the floor in a fit of laughter. Just then her name was called for her appointment. Breathing a sigh of relief she walked past the two girls and sat in the stylists chair. Jade told her what she wanted and the stylist nodded and went to work. She had just finished trimming the back of Jade's hair when one of the girls who was laughing at her earlier took the empty seat next to her.

Jade silently fumed as the girl stared at her through the mirror with a taunting expression on her face. The stylist moved to work on Jade's bangs and she was glad not to be able to see her anymore. She did absolutely nothing to these girls yet here they were, making fun of her.

All of a sudden, the laughter resumed. Jade bit down on her lip, trying not to let it bother her. But she could feel the anger boiling inside her.

She sniffed the air, smelling something odd.

She then heard screams from the chair next to her. Jade whipped her head around to see the commotion, almost getting cut in the eye in the process.

Her mouth fell open at the sight of the girl seated next to

her, her hair on fire. The straightener that was being used on her hair now laid on the floor, melted and mangled.

There is absolutely no way that I caused this, was Jade's first thought. She shook her head, knowing damn well she can't control things like that to happen.

But it would be awesome if she could.

That thought stayed with her for weeks after her appointment, and she noticed similar things would happen when someone would piss her off enough. Something bad would always happen, even if she didn't directly wish for it to happen. That was enough for her to believe.

Lana's love of magic began much earlier than the other two. She had learned a couple years ago that she may have some sort of ability, when she found she was able to move objects with her mind. Not too far, but still able to move them, and she too could make things explode or catch fire or something when her emotions were strong enough.

Lana kept her abilities a secret, fearing what would happen to her if anyone had found out. But she still practiced whenever she could.

"Okay, girls," Lana said as she stopped on a page about a third of the way through the book. "I believe this is the one. This is the spell that will help us out with Veronica. Jade, did you manage to get a lock of her hair?" She asked as Rose bent over to check out the spell herself.

Jade rummaged around in her bag. "I did, and it was a disgusting job. Please don't make me do anything like that ever again." She replied, holding up a plastic bag containing some of Veronica's hair. "She left her brush lying around in the locker room after gym the other day. Made it all too easy for me. Here," she tossed Lana the bag. She set it down next to a large candle.

"Hopefully this is all we'll need," she told them.

"You're not sure?" Rose asked, looking up from the pages she was reading.

Lana shifted uncomfortably. "Well, I"ve never actually attempted anything like this before," she admitted. "But neither have the two of you," she quickly added.

"True." Her friends awkwardly nodded at each other.

Jade clapped her hands and then rubbed them together. "Let's get this started then."

The girls all gathered around the candle. Lana placed the book in the center, so that they could all read it. Placing their left hand on the shoulder of the person next to them, they connected their little circle. In their free hand they each held a few pieces of Veronica's hair.

Softly at first, they began to chant. As they continued their voices grew louder and the pace quickened.

"Place the hair in the fire," Lana instructed. As they laid it in the flame she closed her eyes, saying Veronica's name over and over and chanting something in a language neither Rose nor Jade knew. They threw each other a quick glance but remained silent, as to not ruin Lana's concentration. As she continued to speak, the room began to fill with a light fog, the flames dancing wildly on every single candle across the room. They cast eerie shadows all around them.

As Lana uttered the last syllable her eyes flew open, and at once the flames stopped their dance and the fog disappeared, leaving no trace. It was as if it never existed in the first place.

"Whoa," Rose breathed.

"Yeah," Jade added. "You think it worked?"

Lana closed the book. "Well, we'll have to wait until Monday at school, but I've got a really good feeling about it." She smiled, hugging the book close to her chest.

THREE

The girls arrived extra early to school on Monday, eager to see if their spell had worked.

"Jade, will you stop moving and fidgeting around so much?" Lana complained.

Jade never sat still when she was nervous. She would always bounce all over the place with her nervous energy. Rose was the same way, only when she was excited, not nervous.

"I'm sorry, but I just can't help it," she admitted. "I just want to know if it worked or not."

"Well, we're about to get our chance," Lana pointed. "Because here she comes."

They braced themselves as Veronica pulled into her usual parking space and hopped out of her overly expensive car. She greeted her friends and then together they walked right up to the front of the building.

"You freaks really should be kept hidden behind the school. You make the rest of us look bad," she laughed as she walked past them and into the school.

"Not even a scratch on her. Still has perfect hair, teeth, and body," Jade said in a mocking yet angry tone. "What happened?" She asked, turning to Lana.

Lana shook her head quickly as she grabbed her backpack off the ground. "I'm not sure. I guess it didn't work."

"Well, that sucks," Rose added, disappointed.

"Sure does, " Jade replied. "It's not fair, nothing bad ever happens to her." The three of them sat there in our disappointment until the bell rang.

Nothing bad did happen until about halfway through the school day. The girls were in English class, when suddenly their teacher stopped writing on the blackboard and fainted, hitting her head on the sharp corner of her desk. The class panicked and a few others screamed as someone ran to get the principal and the nurse.

Jade, Lana, and Rose slowly looked at each other with horrified looks on their faces. Mrs Cooper was a favorite teacher of theirs. She had always treated the three of them with respect, and not at all like they were different, or freaks, like the rest of the school did.

The principal soon got on the intercom and announced to the entire school that class was dismissed for the day.

Mrs Cooper had died.

FOUR

"God, I never thought they would let us go." Jade said as they walked out the front doors of the school to freedom. Parents with worried looks on their faces crowded the front of the building, waiting to pick up their kids and make sure they were safe.

Lana pointed to a woman running through the crowd. "Hey Rose," she said, bumping her friend on the shoulder. "Isn't that your mom?" It was strange to see her mom there, as she never picked Rose up from school. Lana had always been the one to give her a ride.

Rose never got a chance to answer. Her mother quickly spotted her and ran faster, tackling her daughter in a hug. "Are you okay?" she asked, panic in her voice as she checked Rose over for any scrapes or bruises or anything.

"Yeah, mom. I'm fine." Rose wiggled out of her mother's grasp.

"What a freak." Veronica sneered as she walked by. Jade glared at her.

Rose's mother tugged on her arm. "Come on, we have to go. Now." She sounded urgent.

"Slow down, mom. I'm okay. And you're starting to worry me."

Her mother turned and looked Rose straight in the face, eyes shining with tears. "But your brother's not," she said tearfully. "I got another call right after I got the one from your school. It was his coach. He's had some sort of football accident. It's pretty serious, and he's in the hospital."

The three girls looked at each other with terrified looks on their faces. Rose's brother, Tyler, was a huge football star. The best at school actually, and he always had scouts after him. He never had any accidents or injuries while playing. In fact, he was usually the one to give the other players an injury.

This was bad. Really, really bad.

Her face pale, Rose silently nodded and followed her mother to the car. They drove off to the hospital so fast they nearly had an accident themselves.

"You don't think . . ." Jade whispered once they were gone.

Lana quickly shook her head. "Of course not. There's no way we could have possibly caused all of this." Yet she didn't sound confident at all. "Besides, we directed the . . ." she lowered her voice, glancing around to make sure no one was listening in on their conversation, "spell at Veronica. If anything were to happen as a result of what we did, she should be the one affected. The only one. But look." she said, pointing to their enemy, who was laughing obnoxiously, tossing her long blonde hair over her shoulder and flirting with any guy that would listen to her. Which pretty much included any guy with a pulse.

"I know," Jade huffed, irritated. "Nothing happened to her. Not even something as small as tripping in the hallway and falling flat on her stupid face." She let out a small laugh. "I would have loved to see that."

"I would have too. But focus," Lana said sternly.

Jade shut right up. "Sorry."

Lana waved off her apology. "We have to figure out what's happening. And fast."

Jade nodded. "Agreed."

"So what do you say we sneak out tonight and read over the spell we used. See if we can figure out where everything went wrong?"

"No," Jade said, shaking her head. "I don't want to go home right now. What if something terrible happened right at my house? I couldn't face it, especially not if we were the cause." She wrapped her arms tightly around herself.

"All right, we can go now. Come on," she said, leading her friend through the mess of people still standing around outside of the school.

Veronica happened to be standing near Lana's car, so they had no choice but to walk past her.

"Where do you think you're going, freaks?" She sure loved to use that word, especially when referring to them. "Don't you think we all know that the three of you are responsible for this mess? I mean, who else would it be?" Everyone around her laughed.

Jade opened her mouth to respond but Lana pulled her away and into the car. "We really don't want to start anything right now," she whispered, trying her best to ignore the laughter and accusing stares all around them.

Jade stared daggers at Veronica until they drove out of sight, wishing she would just burst into flames or something. "I really wish that the spell had worked," she complained. She sat back in her seat and folded her arms across her chest.

Lana chuckled. Me too, she thought. Me too.

She drove to the abandoned house as fast as she could, anxious to figure out this whole mess. She swore she did everything right.

It would have been a huge help to have Rose with them,

but she understood why she couldn't be there right now. She had to be at the hospital with her brother. He would need her.

When they arrived near the house, Lana parked in her usual spot, hidden under a few bent tree branches. They quickly unbuckled their seatbelts and took off towards the abandoned house.

"I'll check the Book of Shadows," Lana said, ducking to miss a low hanging branch.

"Great. And I'll, uh . . ."

"You can be in charge of the phones," Lana offered. "Maybe keep an eye out for any messages from Rose, or any more emergencies we need to be aware of." She hoped that there wouldn't be anything else.

Jade nodded. "Got it."

They hurried through the door, Lana tossing her phone to Jade as she went straight for the book. Even though no one ever dared to ever visit the house she still preferred to keep it hidden.

You can never be too careful.

Jade set the ringers on both phones to a high volume to make sure she didn't miss any incoming call or message, then sat down on the floor. She gently placed the phones in front of her and sat, with her head in her hands, staring at the blank screens. She willed them to stay silent, not sure she could take any more bad news.

Lana located the book and quickly flipped to the page containing the spell they used. She read the whole thing over and over, thinking back to what happened when they cast it. She was sure they pronounced everything correctly, and that they didn't miss or add any unnecessary words. She shook her head, frustrated and confused.

"I don't know!" She yelled in frustration, startling Jade. "I don't know what went wrong. I can't find anything."

"Maybe it wasn't us then?" Jade offered, her voice tinged with hope. She shrugged her shoulders. "We can't be the only witches in town."

Lana looked back down at the opened pages. When she had yelled out she pushed the book away from her a bit, and it now laid at an angle. She squinted. There was some small writing that she was absolutely sure wasn't there before.

Her hand flew to her mouth. Lana slowly looked up to her friend, eyes wide. "It was us," she said in a small, shaky voice.

Jade stood, fear coursing through her. "How do you know?" She asked slowly, not sure if she wanted to know the answer or not based on her friend's expression.

Lana didn't answer, just pointed to the passage that she just discovered.

Jade bent down to see what had freaked Lana out so bad. She located the words, and read them out loud.

"Beware, this spell.
    For it brings dark not light.
    If you are not skilled
    In the art of magic
    You will invite
    Death into your life."

"But what does it mean?" Jade asked. "It doesn't make any sense to me.".

Lana took the book from her. "I'm not entirely sure, but I think it's some kind of warning. That this spell isn't what we initially thought it was. That it will do more harm than good. And not what we intended, which was just to hurt Veronica a little."

Jade threw her hands up in the air. "So, what...are you saying that we just invited death into our world? That it's after us instead of merely playing some stupid trick on Veronica?"

Lana looked up at her friend, fear flashing in her eyes.

"That's exactly what I'm saying."

FIVE

"Oh, my god," Jade said, over and over again as she paced back and forth on the worn carpet. "What are we going to do? This is serious." She turned to Lana, who was still pouring over the Book of Shadows, trying to find a solution, some way to maybe reverse the spell they cast.

Spells can be reversed, right?

"I don't know," Lana answered impatiently, flipping furiously through the pages. "There has to be something though. Something else we missed."

"Like what?" Jade yelled, her voice echoing off the walls. Desperation filled her voice. "We already missed the warning, what more could there possibly be?"

"Like I said, I don't know," Lana replied through clenched teeth, trying to keep her own voice calm. "But I'm going to find it."

"Well hurry, please."

Lana eyed her friend. She knew Jade didn't mean to be so bossy. She was stressed. They all were. This situation was taking a toll on all of them. She shook her head and resumed searching for the hidden answer she was sure had to be there.

It just had to.

Jade got tired of pacing and took to wandering the rest of the house, leaving Lana to read in peace.

After what felt like hours of searching, Lana closed her eyes and rubbed them gently, giving them a break from the strain of staring at page after page. When she opened them again she noticed the room was slowly filling with a thick, black colored smoke. Lana blinked a few times, thinking she was just seeing things in her exhausted state.

But the smoke remained.

"Jade?" She called out. "Jade, you're not smoking again, are you? Or knocking over any candles?" She didn't smoke all that often, but the last time she did Jade almost set the whole place on fire. It didn't help that the abandoned house was filled with leaves and twigs, and made from old rotting wood. Smoking was the last thing she should be doing here.

"Jade?" She called a third time, with a little more urgency.

Still no answer.

Lana was starting to get really worried. With each passing second the smoke grew thicker, filling half the room by now. If there really was a fire she needed to find Jade and get the hell out of here, now.

Before it was too late.

As she looked around she noticed the doorway was completely blocked by the smoke. It was the only way out of the room.

Crap.

Lana sucked in a deep breath, and shielding her eyes with her arm, ran towards the door. Her skin began to burn wherever the smoke came in contact with it. She opened her mouth to scream, and the smoke quickly filled her lungs, burning the entire way down.

Choking, with tears stinging her eyes, Lana fell to her knees. The air near the floor was mostly clear, but it hardly gave her any relief. Even through the pain, she was still determined to find her friend. Clawing her way across the floor, she found herself at the bottom of the stairs. The last time she remembered seeing Jade was when she gave up her pacing and walked up the stairs to the second floor to wander around. Jade never could stay still when she was nervous or anxious.

Lana closed her eyes again and began to drag herself slowly up the stairs. Along with the burning sensation her energy was being drained, fast. She didn't know if she'd be able to make it.

She kept pulling herself up the stairs until she ran into an obstacle. With her eyes still closed due to the massive amount of smoke, she felt around with her hands to see if she could move and maybe identify the object in her way. Whatever it was felt soft, yet heavy.

Prying her eyes open a sliver, she realized the smoke was just too thick to see anything, so she quickly snapped them shut again, feeling them sting a little. She had no choice but to try and crawl over top of it, whatever it was.

As she began to pull herself up and over whatever was blocking the stairs, she stopped short when she felt something familiar - hair. Human hair.

Screams ripped from her raw, burned throat as she realized she had been trying to climb over the body of her best friend. Lana frantically felt around, trying to find a pulse on Jade or some sign that she was still breathing.

Nothing.

She found absolutely no sign of life.

She slumped back against the railing in defeat. She didn't know what to do. She didn't know where she was anymore, let alone how to get out of here. The smoke had completely scrambled her brain.

If she could, Lana would cry. But her insides felt like ash.

"Lana! Jade! Where is everyone?" Rose coughed.

Lana had never been so glad to hear Rose's voice in her life.

When she opened her mouth to yell out to her friend, nothing came out. So she tried banging on the railing to get Rose's attention, but she could barely make a sound with her rapidly declining energy.

"Guys! Where are you? What is all this smoke? Is everyone all right?" Rose sounded panicked now.

Her voice was getting louder, which was a good sign. It meant Rose was getting closer and she would soon be rescued. Lana slid down the stairs towards Rose's voice.

"Oh, my god!" Rose screamed. "What the hell happened to you, Lana?" She asked as her friend slumped down the stairs. Lana had been in the smoke so long that the skin on her face had nearly melted right off.

Rose gagged.

"Where is Jade?" She asked in a panicked voice.

Without saying a word Lana pointed up the stairs. Rose took off her sweater and covered her face with it, hoping to protect herself as she went off in search of her friend.

She didn't know it wouldn't help. Nothing would. Once you spoke those words, and unleashed that dark magic, nothing could help you.

It wouldn't stop until you and everyone you ever loved was dead.

The smoke, having done its job, cleared right up, leaving no trace of its existence.

No one ever did manage to find those three best friends, as they remained a charred, melted mess of skin and bones all down the stairs of that abandoned house.

Let this be a warning to anyone wanting to dabble in dark

magic. It is not kind, it will not do your bidding. You mess with it, and it will mess with you right back.

And will not stop until all is dead.